DREAMWORKS

HOW TO TRAIN YOUR
DRAGON 2

Toothless
A Dragon
Hero's Story

by Erica David
illustrated by Lane Garrison

Simon Spotlight
New York London Toronto Sydney New Delhi

SIMON SPOTLIGHT

An imprint of Simon & Schuster Children's Publishing Division

1230 Avenue of the Americas, New York, New York 10020

How to Train Your Dragon 2 © 2014 DreamWorks Animation L.L.C.

SIMON SPOTLIGHT and colophon are registered trademarks of Simon & Schuster, Inc.

For information about special discounts for bulk purchases, please contact Simon & Schuster Special Sales
at 1-866-506-1949 or business@simonandschuster.com.

Manufactured in the United States of America 0314 PH1

First Edition 10 9 8 7 6 5 4 3 2 1

ISBN 978-1-4814-1928-4

ISBN 978-1-4814-1929-1 (eBook)

The skies above the village of Berk were full of
sunshine. Toothless and his rider, Hiccup, were
soaring through the air, practicing some new flying
tricks. With his injured tail Toothless couldn't fly on his
own, but together the Night Fury and his best
friend, Hiccup, made the perfect team.

Later that day, when Toothless and Hiccup flew farther away from Berk to explore, they came across an enemy ship. The ship's captain, Eret, told them about Drago Bludvist, an evil dragon rider who was building a dragon army to take over the world. "Drago is coming for all your dragons," Eret warned.

Toothless and Hiccup flew home to warn the people of Berk, then set off to find Drago Bludvist. But they soon encountered a mysterious dragon rider. The daring rider captured Hiccup in midair! Without Hiccup to steer his tail, Toothless tumbled into the ocean far below.

The dragon rider took Hiccup to a faraway place called Dragon Mountain. Sea dragons soon brought Toothless to join them. "I'm glad to see you, bud," said Hiccup. Toothless snarled at the dragon rider, but when the rider stretched out a hand toward him, the Night Fury softened.

"Uh, should I know you?" Hiccup asked the dragon rider.

At last the rider took off her mask. Hiccup was stunned. It was his long-lost mother, Valka! Hiccup gasped. "Everyone thinks you were eaten by dragons!"

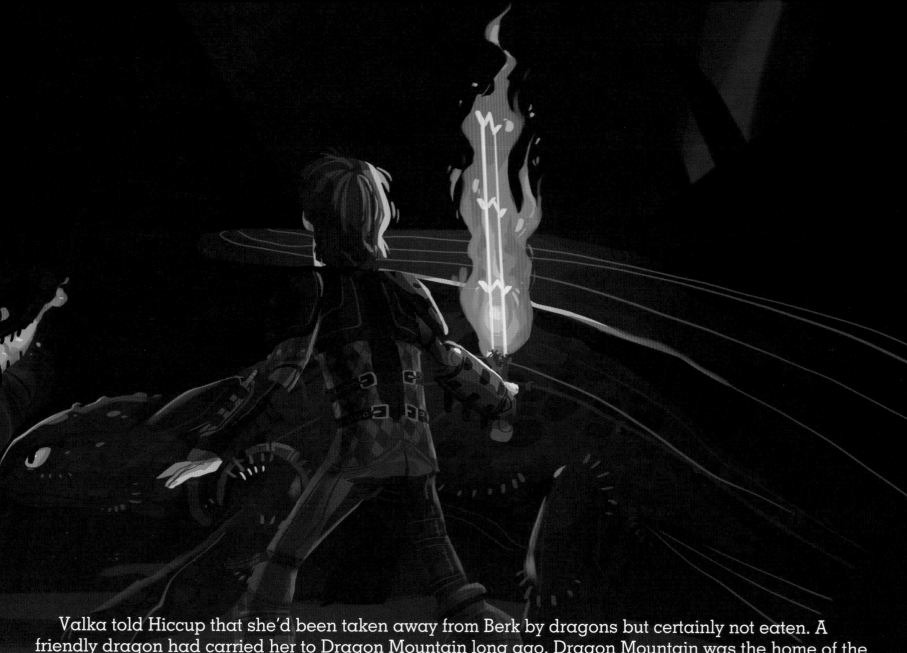

Valka told Hiccup that she'd been taken away from Berk by dragons but certainly not eaten. A friendly dragon had carried her to Dragon Mountain long ago. Dragon Mountain was the home of the great Bewilderbeast.

"The Bewilderbeast is the king of all dragons," explained Valka. "He protects us. We all live under his care, and his command."

Valka showed Toothless and Hiccup around the mountain. She had lived among dragons for a long time and knew a lot about them. She was eager to share what she knew with Hiccup. "Did you know that Toothless is your age? Or that he's quite possibly the last of the Night Furies?" she asked.

Valka gently touched Toothless's back. Toothless snorted softly in surprise. Suddenly, another row of fins stood up along his back and tail, making it easier for him to fly.

"Every dragon has its secrets," Valka said.

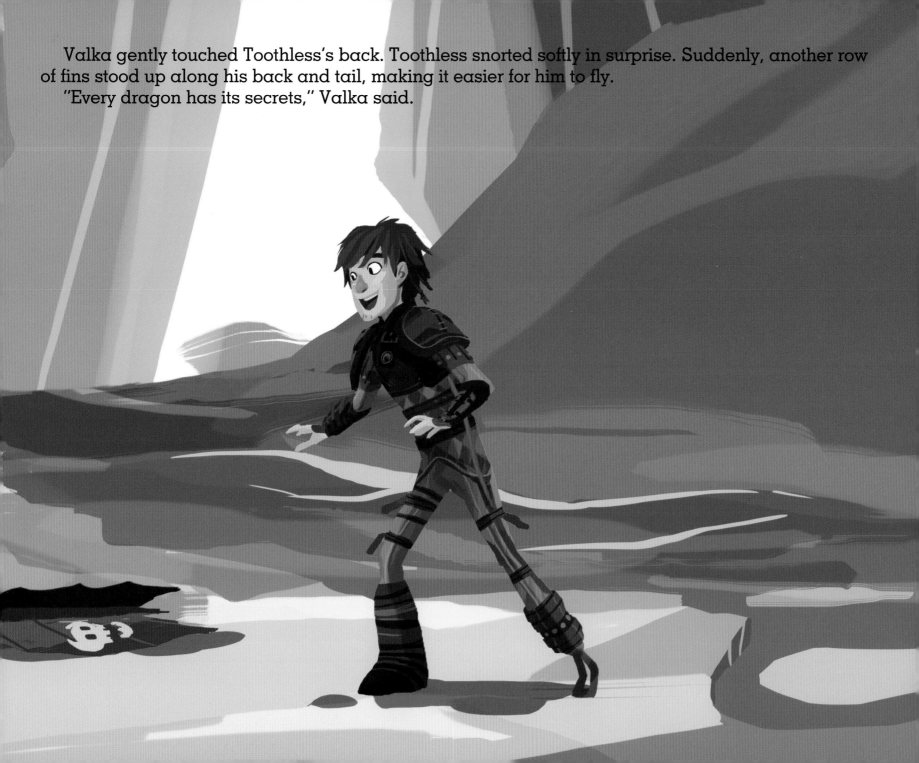

Meanwhile, the villagers of Berk discovered that Toothless and Hiccup had disappeared. Hiccup's father, Chief Stoick, and Gobber flew to Dragon Mountain to rescue them. When Stoick arrived, he was shocked to see that his wife, Valka, was alive!

"You're as beautiful as the day I met you," he told her. Stoick was overjoyed, but there was no time to celebrate.

A loud noise shook Dragon Mountain, and Hiccup and his family raced outside. It was Drago Bludvist and his dragon army! They rose quickly into the air, ready to swoop down and attack. Toothless and the Vikings fought the dragon army bravely, but Drago had a secret weapon—another Bewilderbeast!

This Bewilderbeast was under Drago's control. He battled Valka's Bewilderbeast and defeated him. At Drago's command, his Bewilderbeast made all the dragons on the mountain bow down to him.

"No dragon can resist the alpha's command," Drago said menacingly. "So he who controls the alpha controls them all."

Toothless didn't want to bow to Drago's Bewilderbeast, but the alpha dragon's trance made him. He forced Toothless to bow and even made him send a blast at his best friend, Hiccup!

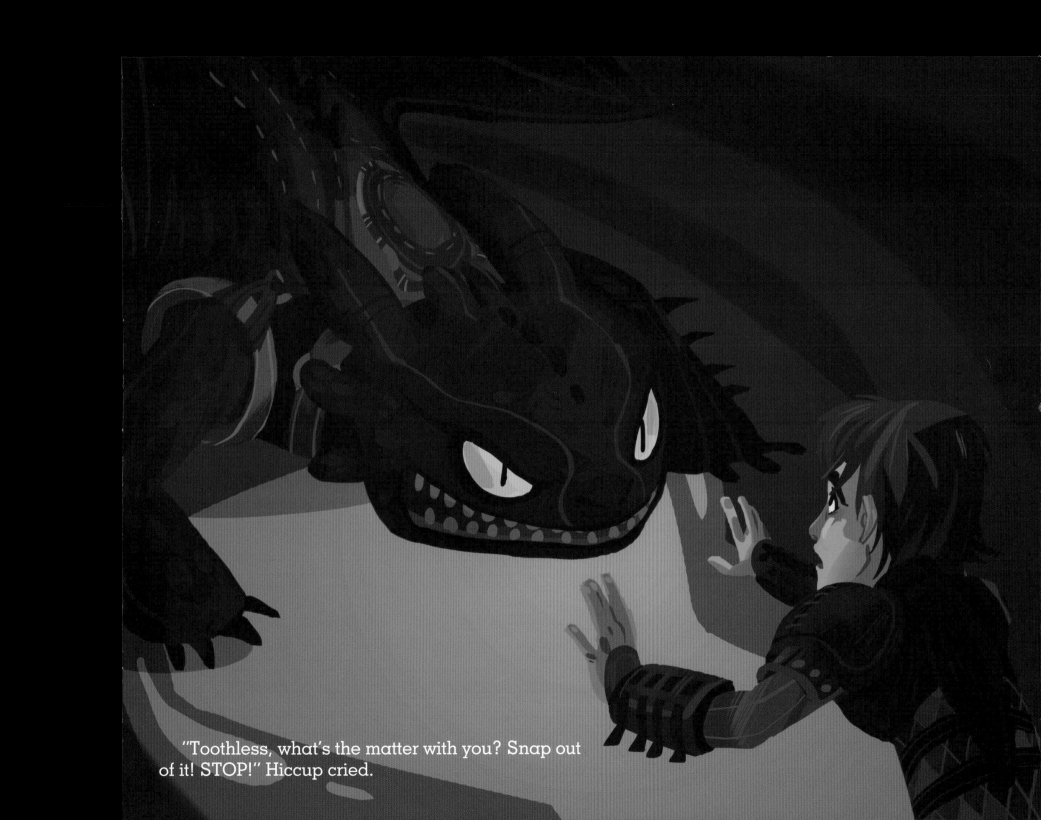

"Toothless, what's the matter with you? Snap out of it! STOP!" Hiccup cried.

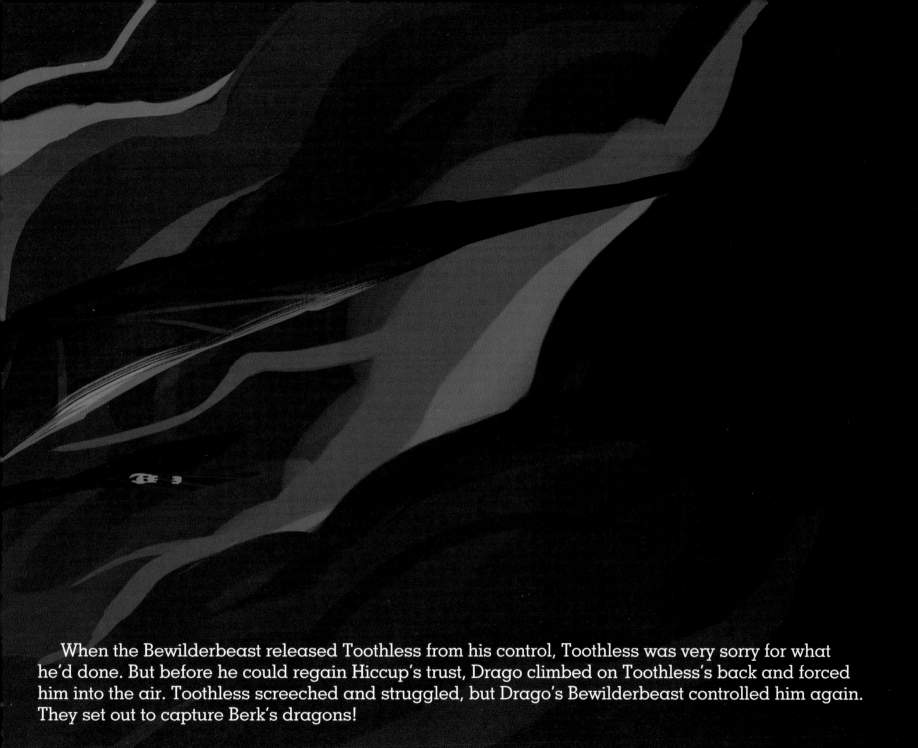

When the Bewilderbeast released Toothless from his control, Toothless was very sorry for what he'd done. But before he could regain Hiccup's trust, Drago climbed on Toothless's back and forced him into the air. Toothless screeched and struggled, but Drago's Bewilderbeast controlled him again. They set out to capture Berk's dragons!

"We have to get Toothless back and stop Drago!" said Hiccup.
He, Valka, and the other Vikings raced toward Berk riding newly hatched baby dragons. The hatchlings were the only dragons that couldn't be controlled by the Bewilderbeast.

Hiccup overtook Drago and Toothless in the skies above Berk. Hiccup was no longer angry at Toothless. He pleaded with Toothless to snap out of his trance.

"It wasn't your fault, bud. They made you do it," Hiccup said gently. "Come back to me."

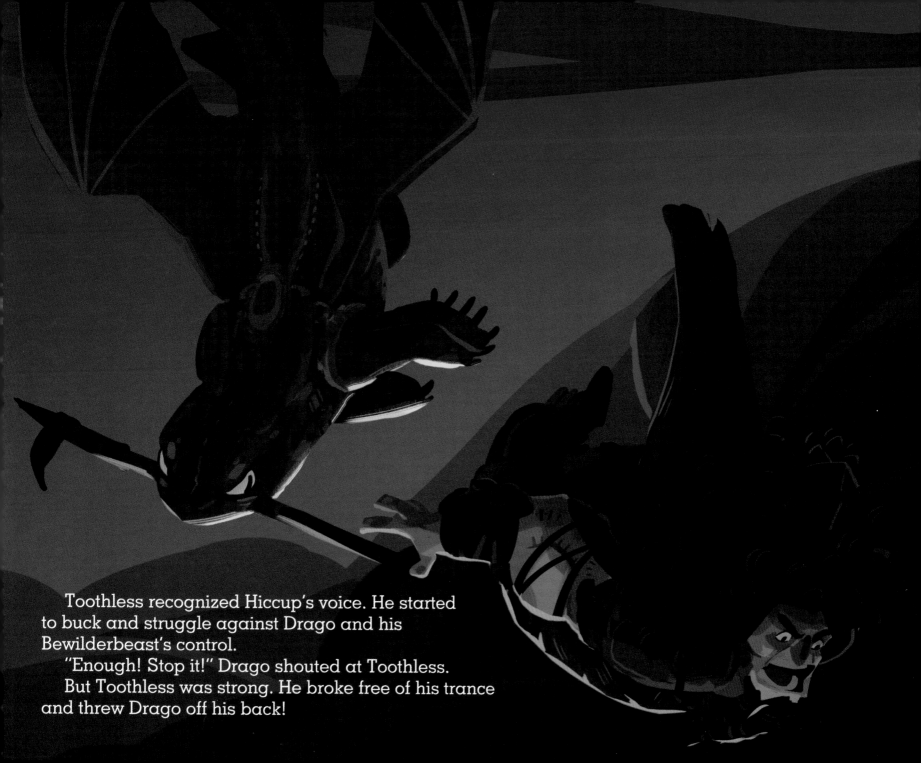

Toothless recognized Hiccup's voice. He started
to buck and struggle against Drago and his
Bewilderbeast's control.

"Enough! Stop it!" Drago shouted at Toothless.

But Toothless was strong. He broke free of his trance
and threw Drago off his back!

Hiccup hopped onto Toothless's back. They were a team again! Together they zoomed straight toward the Bewilderbeast. The alpha was still under Drago's control and it was up to them to stop him!

The Bewilderbeast roared in anger. He reared back and blasted at Toothless and Hiccup, freezing them in a block of ice!

But the ice wasn't strong enough to hold Toothless. With a Night Fury fire blast, he shattered the ice and burst free!

Toothless charged toward the Bewilderbeast, firing and hitting the alpha dragon right in the face. "He's challenging the alpha!" exclaimed Hiccup. "He's doing it to protect you," said Valka.

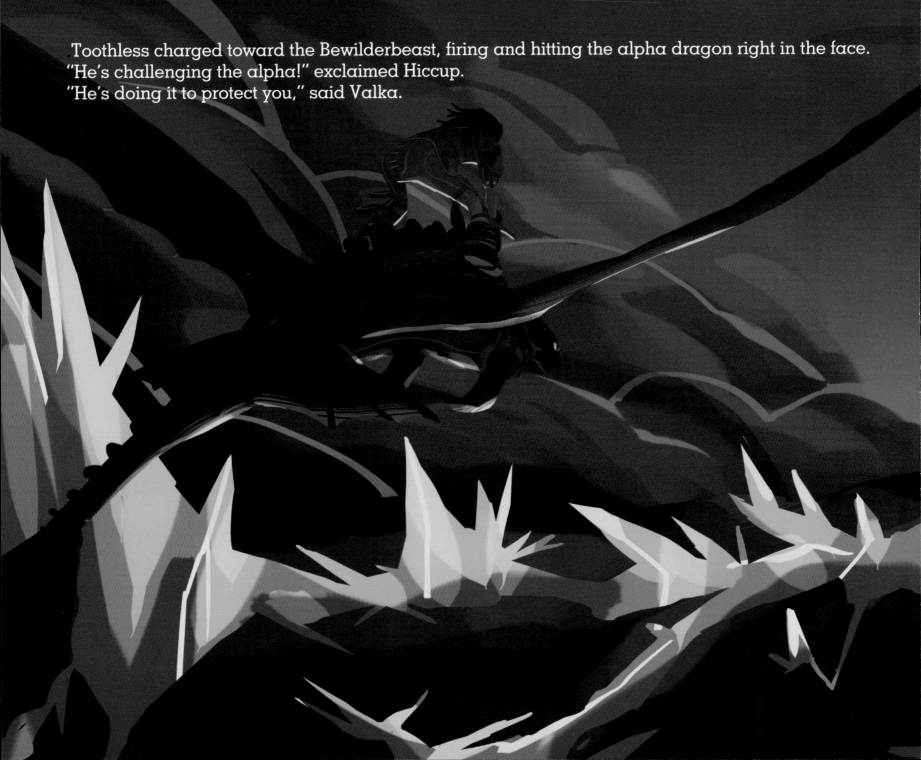

"Fight back!" Drago screamed at his Bewilderbeast.
The Bewilderbeast bellowed and raged, but Toothless
didn't give up. He blasted the Bewilderbeast with
fireballs and drove him to surrender into the icy water.

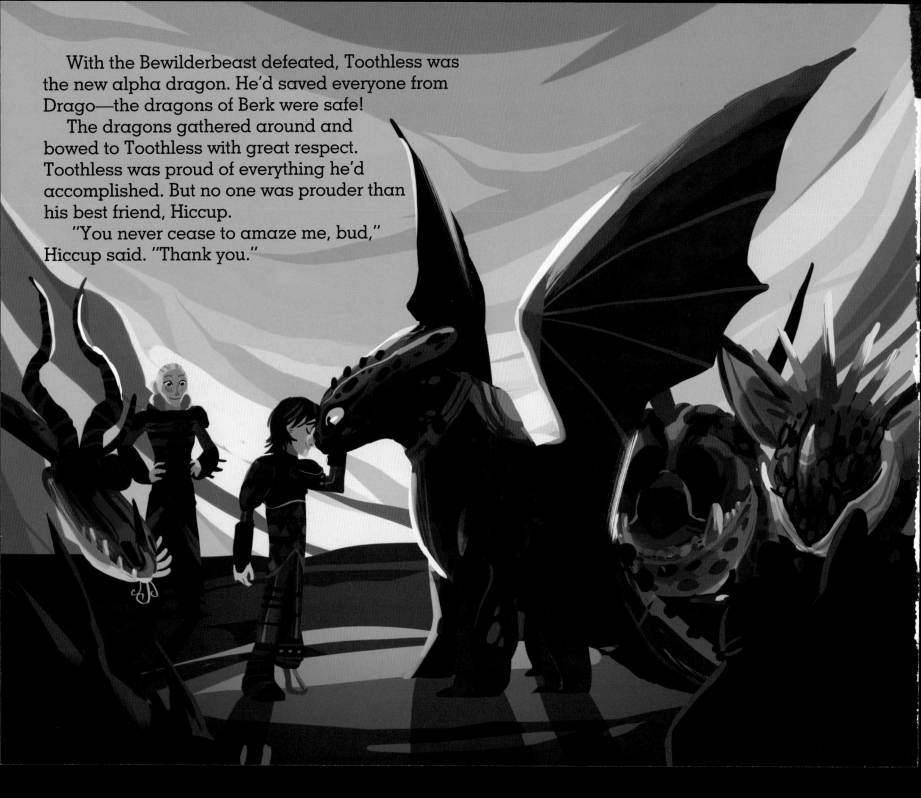

With the Bewilderbeast defeated, Toothless was the new alpha dragon. He'd saved everyone from Drago—the dragons of Berk were safe!

The dragons gathered around and bowed to Toothless with great respect. Toothless was proud of everything he'd accomplished. But no one was prouder than his best friend, Hiccup.

"You never cease to amaze me, bud," Hiccup said. "Thank you."